KU-104-464

ACC. No: 07085892

For Caroline and Matt Walker, with much love xxx
E.D.

For Erin and Luke
L.D.

Quarto is the authority on a wide range of topics.
Quarto educates, entertains and enriches the lives of
our readers—enthusiasts and lovers of hands-on living.
www.quartoknows.com

Text by Elizabeth Dale
Illustrations by Liam Darcy

© 2021 Quarto Publishing plc

This edition first published in 2021 by Happy Yak,
an imprint of The Quarto Group.
The Old Brewery, 6 Blundell Street,
London N7 9BH, United Kingdom.
T (0)20 7700 6700 F (0)20 7700 8066
www.QuartoKnows.com

All rights reserved. No part of this publication may be reproduced, stored
in a retrieval system, or transmitted in any form or by any means, electronic,
mechanical, photocopying, recording, or otherwise, without the prior
permission of the publisher, nor be otherwise circulated in any form of
binding or cover other than that in which it is published and without a
similar condition being imposed on the subsequent purchaser.

A catalogue record for this book is available from the British Library.

ISBN 978 0 7112 5960 7

Manufactured in Guangzhou, China EB042021

9 8 7 6 5 4 3 2 1

Delightfully Different
DILLY

ELIZABETH DALE   LIAM DARCY

All the penguins loved living together
in their beautiful snowy home.

They loved sliding on the ice, swimming
through the waves and huddling together
when icy winds blew.

They loved that they all looked the same
and waddled in the same funny way.

They were one huge, noisy family...

Especially when their eggs hatched
and the chicks joined in!

When Dilly hatched, her mummy and
daddy couldn't have loved her more.

From the top of her fluffy head to
the bottom of her tiny foot.

"Isn't she just perfect?!"
said Dilly's mummy, proudly.

"Absolutely!" agreed Dilly's Daddy.

And she was!

When the parents went hunting, Dilly
played with the other baby penguins.

But they noticed something
different about her.

"She doesn't waddle like us," said Pip.
"She hops," said Popple.
"Penguins don't hop!" said Sue.

"I do!" said Dilly. "I'm different. Hopping is fun. You should try it!"

So the other baby penguins all tried hopping.

It was very hard!
And they weren't
very good at it.

They tripped,
and slipped
and slid.

None of them
could get it right...

Though some
landings were softer
than others!

"How do you do it,
Dilly?" asked Pip.

"I only have one leg," said Dilly.
"So I use it all the time and it's lovely
and strong. Look!"

Dilly could hop
from one ice floe
to another...

... and over a penguin... or two!

She could twirl round and round – fast!

Everyone tried Dilly's tricks. They weren't very good at them.

But they had fun!

"What else do you do differently?" Popple asked.
"Look and copy me!"
Dilly replied.

Sometimes hopping was better!

But sometimes it was much harder.

So Dilly found new ways to do things.

When the parents came back,
some found it hard to find their babies.

They all looked the same...
apart from Dilly.

She was always easy to spot!

But the other mummies and
daddies worried about Dilly.

"She's not like us,"
one said, frowning.

"She doesn't waddle!"
said another.

"And she's teaching our babies
odd things," said another.

"Stop being different, Dilly!" the mummies and daddies all cried.

Poor Dilly was very sad.

Dilly stopped twirling, roly-polying and hopping.

She did tiny twisty hops, hoping that they looked like waddles.

But she couldn't keep up with the other babies.

'Wait!' cried Pip and Popple, as they grabbed a flipper each and helped Dilly up the slope.

They'd just reached
the top when...

AHHHHHHHH!

AHHHHHH!

They all went slippy-sliding back down...
straight into a snow hole!

"Help! Help!" they all called.

Popple's mummy heard her calling
but she couldn't see her.

"Popple, darling, where are you?"
she called.

"Down here!" wailed
Popple, starting to cry.

"I can't see you!" called
her mummy.

"We're here!" called Dilly, and she
hopped as high as she could.
And Popple's mummy saw her!

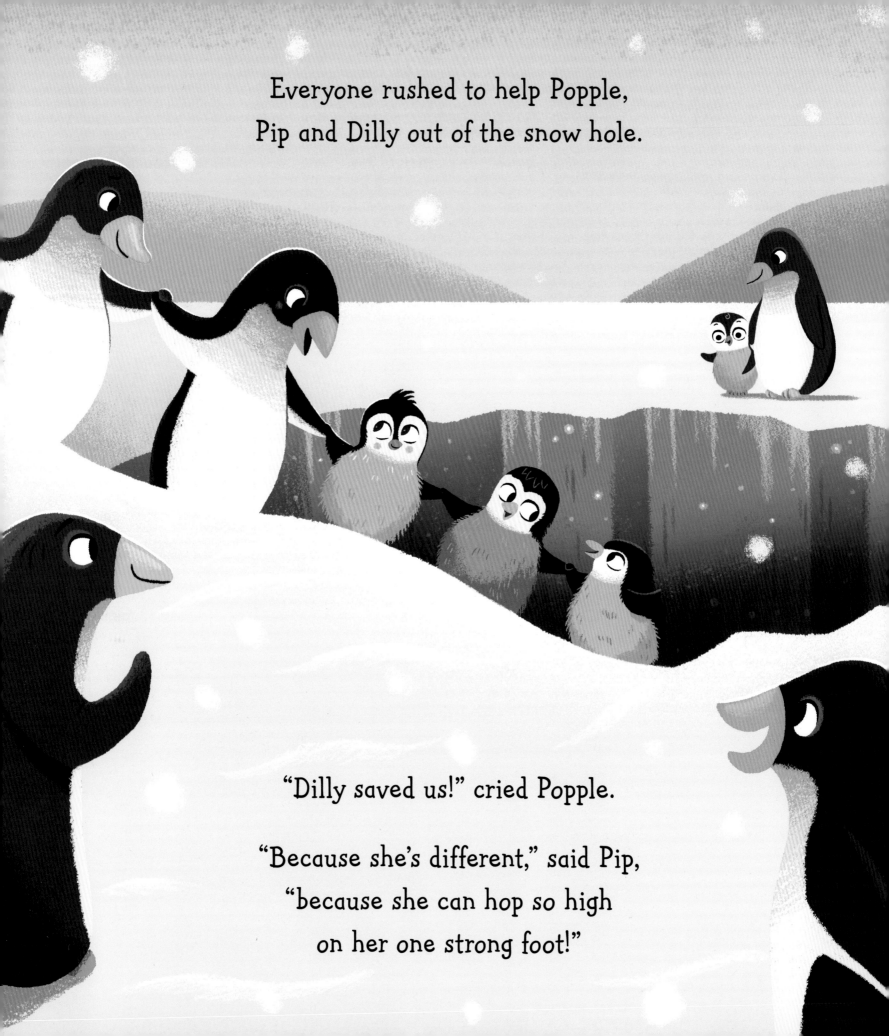

Everyone rushed to help Popple,
Pip and Dilly out of the snow hole.

"Dilly saved us!" cried Popple.

"Because she's different," said Pip,
"because she can hop so high
on her one strong foot!"

"Thank you, Dilly!" Popple and Pip's
mummies said, hugging her.

"We're so sorry. It seems it's good to
be different," said Popple's daddy.

"Yes, maybe we could all do with
a little change," said Pip's daddy.

So from that day on, sometimes the penguins did things a little differently.

Some liked to twirl, slow... and fast!

Some liked to do funny dives and big hops.

And they all liked
to do roly-polys!

"Being different
is brilliant!" they all cried.

"Thank you, Dilly!"